D0386764

The Case of the Snack Snatcher

For misfit detectives everywhere—*Liam*

To my dad, my family, and with special thanks to Laurent—*Aurélie*

West Meadows Detectives

The Case of the Snack Snatcher

Written by
Liam O'Donnell

Illustrated by
Aurélie Grand

Owlkids Books

Owlkids Books acknowledges the financial support of the Canada Council for the
Arts, the Ontario Arts Council, the Government of Canada through the Canada
Book Fund (CBF) and the Government of Ontario through the Ontario Media
Development Corporation's Book Initiative for our publishing activities.

Published in Canada by
Owlkids Books Inc.
10 Lower Spadina Avenue
Toronto, ON M5V 2Z2

Published in the United States by
Owlkids Books Inc.
1700 Fourth Street
Berkeley, CA 94710

Library and Archives Canada Cataloguing in Publication

O'Donnell, Liam, 1970-, author
        The case of the snack snatcher / Liam O'Donnell ; illustrated by Aurélie Grand.

(West Meadows Detectives 1) ISBN 978-1-77147-069-8 (bound)

        I. Grand, Aurélie, illustrator   II. Title.

PS8629.D64C38 2015   jC813'.6   C2014-908455-2

Library of Congress Control Number: 2015934527

Edited by: Karen Li
Designed by: Claudia Dávila

Manufactured in Altona, MB, Canada, in April 2015, by Friesens Corporation
Job #210619

A   B   C   D   E   F

Publisher of Chirp, chickaDEE and OWL
www.owlkidsbooks.com

Table of Contents

CHAPTER 1

Everything was new. New shirt. New shoes. New school.

I don't like new.

"Hurry up, Myron!" Mom shouted from the edge of the schoolyard. She was not new. The screaming baby in her arms? Totally new. Sofia, my baby sister. She's eight months old. When a baby is eight months old, it is still new. So I guess I should say she's eight months new. When it's a baby, it cries a lot. And that gets old really fast.

I stood at the school gates. I crossed my arms.

"Stop digging your heels into the sidewalk," Mom said. "Let's go!"

I wasn't really digging my heels into the sidewalk. That would be impossible. The sidewalk is made of concrete. My heels are made of skin, bone, muscles, and blood. And I only had running shoes on. It was an expression. I don't like expressions, either.

Expressions are when someone says one thing and means another thing. For example, when people say, "I'm feeling blue today," they don't mean their skin has turned blue. They mean they're sad. Why don't they just say, "I'm sad"? Expressions are confusing. They are not the truth. The truth is very important to detectives like me.

"Mom, can I go, please? I see Tianna from camp."

That was my sister Alicia. She's in eighth grade and is always happy to have something new. New shoes, new backpack, new hairdo. She waved to a group of girls near the bike racks. They waved back. The first day of school and she already had a new group of friends.

"Go ahead," Mom said. "But remember to check in on Myron at lunch."

Alicia scrunched up her face at me. That was a scowl. It meant she wasn't happy.

"He's in third grade! He's not a baby anymore, Mom," she said.

Mom dropped her own scowl on Alicia. I'm not too good at picking up on people's expressions, but I had seen that scowl from

Mom since I was Sofia's age. So had Alicia. It meant: Don't mess with me.

"Fine," Alicia said. She stomped into the schoolyard.

Which just left me.

Mom stuck a pink plastic soother into Sofia's mouth. My sister stopped screaming and started sucking on the thing.

"Myron, I'm sorry we had to move away from your old school and your friends," Mom said. "But we're still in Whispering Meadows. You can visit them on the weekends. Your new school is going to be fun."

West Meadows Elementary did not look like fun. It had a big field with soccer nets, a basketball court, and a red-and-yellow climbing frame. Sure, all that stuff sounds fun, but the playground was crawling with kids I didn't know. That made my brain itch.

"Mr. Harpel said we could go straight in and see him," Mom said. She held out her pinkie finger. "You met him last week, remember?"

Mr. Harpel was my new teacher, and he seemed nice. And room 15 was unlike any classroom I'd had before. The itch in my brain faded.

I took a deep breath, wrapped my pinkie around Mom's, and took my first steps into my new school.

Room 15

Mr HARPEL

CHAPTER 2

Mr. Harpel greeted us at the door.

"Welcome, welcome, welcome to room 15, Myron!" His voice was loud. He was tall and round. He had a bushy beard and shiny shoes. His shoes had no laces. My shoes don't have laces, either. Laces come loose and then my shoes slip off my feet. I wondered if Mr. Harpel had the same problem.

Mom squeezed my pinkie. "I'll pick you up at the end of the day."

I squeezed back. Mom left.

Mr. Harpel smiled at me.

"Welcome, Myron! Come in."

"Four," I said.

"Sorry?" Mr. Harpel said.

"You said 'welcome' four times," I said. When someone says something over and over again, it's called repeating. People repeat themselves when they are really serious or really nervous. Good detectives always notice when people repeat themselves.

"You're right." He laughed. "I guess I want you to feel very welcome. You're the first one to arrive. You've got the place to yourself."

Everyone called my new classroom room 15. That's because there was a sign on the door that said "Room 15."

I had visited room 15 with Mom and Dad last week, before school started. It wasn't like a regular classroom. There were no desks in rows and no chalkboard at the front. It was like a living room. There was a couch in one corner with cushions. The carpet had red and yellow circles. Against one wall, there was a bookcase packed with books and board games. A round table stood in the center of the room. There were also four desks—one for each student in the class.

Room 15 was not my only classroom. In the afternoon I would go to a different one. It was called my "regular classroom." I visited that room last week, too. It had desks and a chalkboard. It also had more kids. And it had another teacher—Ms. Chu. She was old. She was probably a grandmother.

I wanted to stay in room 15 all day, but Mom said I needed to be in Ms. Chu's classroom sometimes. Ms. Chu's classroom did not have couches. It would have other children. Children I did not know. Thinking about Ms. Chu's class got my brain itching again.

Mr. Harpel put an orange folder on each of the desks in room 15.

"Today, Myron, we're just going to get to know each other," he said. "We'll play some games and—"

"Aaaaaahh!" A shrill scream outside the classroom made us both jump.

"What was *that*?" Mr. Harpel said.

I followed him into the hallway.

"The scream sounded like it came from that room down the hall," I said.

"That's the kitchen. Good hearing, Myron."

"My dad says I have better hearing than an

owl," I said. "That's impossible, but he means I hear very well. Did you know that an owl can use its ears to pinpoint the exact location of a mouse in under a second?"

"I didn't know that."

I was going to tell Mr. Harpel more about owls, because I like them and know a lot about them. For instance, they swallow their prey whole and then throw up the bones and fur. These are called owl pellets, and you can find them if you walk in the forest where owls live.

I didn't tell Mr. Harpel this because he had gone into the kitchen and would not have heard me. I followed him.

The room looked like a kitchen made for twins. There were two of everything. There were two stoves, two fridges, two microwave

ovens, and two sinks. Two metal tables stood in the middle of the room. They were covered in food. Uncooked pasta spilled out from ripped-open bags. Shredded cheddar cheese coated the floor. White flour lay in piles on the table and was spread across the floor.

In all that mess stood the school chef. Her apron was stained with red splotches and white flour smears. She wore an earring shaped like a little yellow school bus in each ear. The school bus on her left ear was upside down, so the wheels were pointing to the sky instead of the ground.

"Everything all right, Mrs. Peterson?" Mr. Harpel asked the woman with the school-bus earrings.

I thought that was a strange question. Mrs. Peterson would not have screamed if everything were all right. Clearly something was not right. But sometimes people—even teachers—ask silly questions.

"Everything is most definitely not all right," Mrs. Peterson replied. "I had the morning snack laid out on the table, ready for the kids. I stepped out of the room for a minute, and when I got back, this is what I found!"

She waved her hand at the food splattered all over the kitchen.

"Whoever did this made a real mess," Mr. Harpel said.

"That mess was going to be lunch. But I can clean that up," said Mrs. Peterson. "I'm upset about the morning snacks. They're gone. We've been robbed!"

CHAPTER 3

The school kitchen was a mess. It was also a crime scene.

The floor was covered in crushed pasta, shredded cheese, and spilled flour.

There were footprints in the flour. They matched the size of Mrs. Peterson's shoes. She must have walked through the mess before we got here.

"You ruined it, Mrs. Peterson," I said.

"Excuse me?" Mrs. Peterson crossed her arms in front of her chest.

"You ruined the evidence with your footprints when you walked through the flour," I said. "Crime scenes need to be left untouched for a mystery to be solved."

"Well, I'm very sorry for that."

"Were you baking with licorice?" I asked.

"Licorice? The candy?" Mrs. Peterson said. "Why would I be using licorice to make macaroni and cheese? And why so many questions?"

"Myron is a detective," Mr. Harpel said.

"Is he a magician, too? Because I need someone to make my morning snacks reappear."

"I am not a magician," I said. "But I can tell you the thief was eating licorice."

Mrs. Peterson stared at the mess on the table and floor.

"I don't see any candy, Mr. Detective," she said.

"I don't either," I said. "But I can smell it. Can't you?" Mr. Harpel and Mrs. Peterson shook their heads. Not surprising. No one can ever smell the things I do. Just like they never hear the things I hear. Mom says I have superpowered senses. I can hear which radio station the neighbor three yards over is listening to on a summer day. I can tell when Sofia needs her diaper changed, even if she's in the other room. As far as superpowers go, I would rather have X-ray vision.

A large shadow fell across the doorway to the kitchen.

"What's going on? I heard a scream. Is everyone okay?"

It was Principal Rainer. She was thin and wrinkled and wore thick shoes with laces.

"We're okay," Mrs. Peterson said. "But we've been robbed."

"Start from the beginning," I said.

Principal Rainer looked at me. "Hello, Myron. Are you enjoying your first day at West Meadows Elementary?"

"I am," I said. "And I'm going to solve this mystery."

"Myron is a detective, Principal Rainer," Mr. Harpel said.

"Is he now?" Principal Rainer chuckled. "Perhaps you should go back to your class, Myron." She turned to Mr. Harpel and raised her eyebrows. "I have an idea who is behind this mess."

"It's okay," I said. "I'll stay and help."

"Myron, we should listen to Principal Rainer and go back to our classroom," Mr. Harpel said.

"I won't be able to solve the mystery from the classroom." I walked farther into the kitchen. I stopped by a wooden door in the far wall. The smell of licorice was suddenly very strong.

"What's in here?"

Mrs. Patterson shrugged. "It's a closet. Just my coat."

The door burst open. A small girl jumped out of the closet.

"And me!" the girl said. She tumbled through the mess on the floor and jumped to her feet. She held her arms out wide like a gymnast.

"Hajrah!" Mrs. Patterson said.

"*Chef* Hajrah here!" she announced. "Ready to take your order." Hajrah wore an apron that was too big for her and a chef's hat that

slipped down her forehead. She ran up to Principal Rainer with one hand held out flat like a notepad. In her other hand, she held a black stick and used it like a pencil.

"Licorice!" I said. That's why I'd smelled the candy.

"Hajrah, what are you doing here?" Principal Rainer said.

"Taking your order for lunch!" Hajrah said. "What will it be?"

"This isn't the time for your games." Principal Rainer scowled.

Hajrah nodded. "Just water for the principal. No problem."

She ran over to Mr. Harpel.

"Howdy, Mr. Harpel. What can I get you?"

"You make an excellent chef, Hajrah, but we're trying to solve a mystery."

"A mystery!" Hajrah said. "I love mysteries! Who's playing the role of the sleuth?"

"I am," I said. "My name is Myron. I'm a detective."

"Awesome!" Hajrah pulled the chef's hat from her head and spun around to face me. Her long, dark braid spun with her. She caught it in one hand, pushed it back over her right shoulder, and grinned. "I'll be your detective partner."

"I don't want a partner," I said. My brain began to itch. "I work alone."

"No problem. We'll work alone together. Like a team!"

"I don't like teams," I said. I scratched my head but couldn't get to the itch under my scalp. Hajrah was going to ruin everything. This mystery was the only good thing to happen at my new school. Now I was stuck on a team I didn't sign up for. I was not good at teams. Hajrah was not good at taking no for an answer. She turned to Principal Rainer.

"We accept the case! West Meadows Detective Agency at your service."

Hajrah took a deep bow, as if she were onstage at the school holiday concert. No one clapped.

She stuffed the rest of her licorice into her mouth, put her arm around me, and pulled me in close for a hug.

"This mystery-solving stuff is going to be so much fun!" she said between licorice chews.

CHAPTER 4

There was a lot of grumbling that morning.
Most of it from stomachs. Turns out Mrs.
Peterson is a super chef and many kids were
looking forward to her morning snacks. She
had nothing to offer but a few treats left over
from summer vacation.

We sat in a circle on the carpet in room 15,
quietly munching stale granola bars. Mr. Harpel
took attendance. It didn't take long. There
were only four kids in the whole class. And
one person was missing.

"Hajrah?" Mr. Harpel looked up from the red attendance folder.

Hajrah jumped to her feet and saluted. "Sir, yes, sir!" She bounced back on her butt.

"Thank you, Hajrah," Mr. Harpel said. "Jordan?"

Jordan didn't answer. He picked at a hole in the leg of his jeans and mumbled something I couldn't understand. He was in fourth grade. I'd known him less than fifteen minutes, and already I'd seen him pick something off his shirt and eat it. I wasn't sure if he did that all the time or was just doing it because Mrs. Peterson's morning snacks had been stolen. Either way, I didn't sit beside him.

"Myron? Are you here?" Mr. Harpel said.

I didn't answer. Mr. Harpel knew I was there. I had just investigated a crime scene

in the kitchen with him. I was sitting right
in front of him. Why did he want to know
if I was here? He could see me, couldn't he?
Maybe he'd suddenly lost his vision?

Mr. Harpel smiled. "Sorry, Myron. Of course
you're here. It's just that some people get
upset if they don't get a chance to say 'Here!'
when I call their names."

"I am not one of those people," I said.

"Thank you for letting me know." Mr. Harpel closed the attendance folder.

"Wait!" Hajrah jumped to her feet. "You forgot Glitch!"

"Do you mean Danielle?" Mr. Harpel said.

"Yeah, but she calls herself Glitch," Jordan mumbled.

"Ah, yes! Glitch." Mr. Harpel wrote something in the attendance folder. "It's all right. I saw Danielle—er, Glitch—already. She'll be here soon." He waved the attendance folder. "Okay, who wants to take the attendance to the office?"

"Myron and me!" Hajrah shouted. She snatched the attendance folder out of Mr. Harpel's hands and dashed to the door. "Let's go, Myron!"

I stayed in my spot in the circle.

"You don't have to go if you don't want to,"
Mr. Harpel said.

Hajrah bounced at the door. "I think you
should come with me. You never know what
clues we'll turn up."

I'm not good at getting hints, but it was
hard to miss this one. Besides, she had a point.
I was on a case. I had a snack thief to catch. I
wouldn't do it sitting in the classroom.

I grabbed my notebook from my desk and
followed her out the door. Detectives carry
notebooks to keep track of clues and suspects.

The hallways outside the class were quiet.
All the kids were in their rooms getting to
know each other and finding out what they'd
be learning this year. I was more interested in
learning about our Snack Snatcher.

Hajrah didn't walk down the corridor—she

zipped. She had
one speed: fast.
She did not zip
in a straight line.
She carved high-
speed curves down
the hallway, like a
downhill skier.
And she talked the
whole way.

"You know why I'm in room 15, Myron?"
she said as she carved another curve in front
of me. "I bounce around too much. That's
what my mom says. And my second-grade
teacher last year. Bounce, bounce, bounce."

I plotted a straight line down the middle
of the hallway. Kids like to hang out and
chat on the edges of hallways, so walking in

the middle gives you the best chance of not crashing into them. Hajrah and I had the hall to ourselves. But you can never tell. If there was a fire drill, this place would be full of kids in seconds.

"What about you?" Hajrah zoomed back. She had her arms out wide and made a noise like an airplane. She circled around me.

"Come on, Myron! If we're going to be detective partners, we have to know each other. Why are you in room 15?"

Hajrah made another airplane circle and stopped in front of me. She smiled with her arms still open wide, just like Sofia when she wakes up from a long nap. Hajrah was not my sister, but she seemed nice.

"I'm autistic," I said. "My brain works differently."

Hajrah wiggled her fingers. Her smile grew bigger. "That will make you a really good detective!"

"My mom says that, too." I matched Hajrah's smile with my own.

Hajrah shrugged and zoomed away down the hallway, still buzzing like an airplane.

We turned a corner and saw the main office right in front of us.

Principal Rainer stood outside the office. She was talking to a tall girl with short curly hair. The girl wore a black jacket, orange jeans, and a backpack covered tiny metal buttons. Hajrah dove behind the trophy case. She pulled me in beside her.

"That's Danielle!" she whispered.

I leaned around the trophy case to get a better look. The buttons on her backpack had pictures of flying robots and spaceships.

"Everyone calls her Glitch because she's really good with computers," Hajrah said.

I did not understand this. A glitch is when something does not work. When my dad cannot get our computer to work, he says there is a "glitch" and tells me to go outside and play, even if I don't want to.

I wondered if Danielle liked being called Glitch. I was going to ask, but Hajrah told me to be quiet. We could hear Principal Rainer speaking.

"I'm going to ask you one more time, Danielle. I expect the truth," Principal Rainer said. "Did you take the snacks from the kitchen?"

"No!" Glitch said. "I just got here."

Hajrah whispered, "Last year, Glitch was

caught taking stuff from people's backpacks."

"Principal Rainer said she had an idea who was behind the thefts," I said.

I flipped open my notebook and wrote down Danielle's name and her nickname.

Principal Rainer and Glitch were done talking. Glitch walked toward us. Her face was scrunched up as if she'd just eaten a lemon.

Hajrah held up the attendance folder so it blocked our faces. "Don't let her see us!"

I peered over the attendance folder. Glitch walked right by us and turned the corner. She didn't even look in our direction.

"That was close!" Hajrah said. "She looked mad enough to shoot lasers from her eyes. You don't want to be near Glitch when she gets mad. Trust me."

I wrote the word "angry" beside Glitch's name in my notebook. Then I put a question mark beside that. Why was she so mad? Did she take the snacks from the kitchen? I had a lot of questions. But now I had something else, too.

I had my first suspect.

CHAPTER 5

The rest of the morning my brain was stuck
on my first suspect: Glitch.

Even if the stories about her were true, it
didn't mean she took the morning snacks. I
planned on talking to her, but Mr. Harpel kept
us pretty busy all morning with activities.

Glitch didn't join us for any of them. She
sat in her corner of the room, poking at a little
metal box with a screwdriver. She didn't say
a word to anyone.

Mr. Harpel said we all needed our own

space sometimes. That's why we each had
our own area in room 15.

Hajrah had a big ball to sit on and a bunch
of toys she could squeeze when she got too
"bouncy." Jordan's corner had a regular desk,
but Mr. Harpel also gave him a bunch of cool
markers and colored pens so he could draw
cars and sports and all the other stuff that he

liked. Glitch's space had a wide table instead of a desk. On the table were little drawers filled with wires, plugs, and other bits of electronics. My area of the room had a small desk with shelves for my mystery books and schoolbooks. There were already a few mystery stories on the shelves. Mr. Harpel had taken them from the library for me.

I was reading about a detective called Encyclopedia Brown. An encyclopedia is a book filled with information. This detective got his nickname because he was smart and knew so much. I was on my second mystery when the lunch bell rang.

"That's it for today, folks!" Mr. Harpel said. "After lunch, you'll go to your regular classes."

Hajrah groaned. "Not Ms. Chu! The chairs

in her class are *so* hard. And she makes me sit still for a million hours!"

"Hajrah, that's a bit of an exaggeration," Mr. Harpel said. "Ms. Chu is a nice teacher. And Myron is in your class. I'm sure she'll let you work together. I teach the older students upstairs in the afternoon, so I'll still be in the school. Maybe you will see me in the hall. If not, I will see you here in room 15 tomorrow morning."

The lunchroom was crowded and loud. I do not like crowded and loud. But I do like lunch. My dad says that sometimes you have to take a bit of what you don't like to get a bit of what you do like. He calls it a compromise.

I don't like compromise.

Hajrah had been through all this before. She led me to the far corner of the room, where it wasn't so busy. A few kids sat quietly eating their lunches.

"Nobody likes eating this far from the exit," she said. "They like to sit close to the doors. Anything to cut down on the time it takes to get outside for recess."

Hajrah started eating her lunch. I pulled out mine, too. It was Monday, so it was a raspberry jam sandwich. I chewed my sandwich and thought about the mystery of the Snack Snatcher.

"Okay, so Glitch is totally the snack thief," Hajrah said.

"We don't know that," I said.

"Who else could it be? Glitch has taken stuff

before, and Principal Rainer thinks it was her."

"*You* were hiding in the cupboard," I pointed out. I had met my detective partner only a few hours ago. For all I knew, she could be the Snack Snatcher.

"I always hide in the cupboard," she said with a shrug. "I got there before Mrs. Peterson arrived. I was supposed to be at the daycare. You know, the one down the hall from the school kitchen? My mom starts work early in the morning, so she drops me off there before school. But the daycare doesn't have cupboards. Cupboards are dark, cozy, and private. They're perfect for eating licorice."

"Then you were there when the Snack Snatcher struck," I said. "Did you see anything?"

"Nope. I was too busy enjoying my

delicious candy. But I did hear a whole bunch of crashing and banging."

"And you didn't open the door to look?"

"No way," Hajrah said. "I thought it was Lindsay looking for me. She works in the daycare and doesn't like it when I sneak off."

"So you hid in the closet the whole time?"

"I was eating licorice. Nothing disturbs me when I'm eating licorice. Remember that, Myron."

I didn't see why I had to remember the eating habits of my detective partner. At that moment, I was more worried about the person staring at me from across the lunchroom.

"Oh no," I said through a mouthful of sandwich.

"Oh no, what?" Hajrah said.

A red-haired girl walked straight up to us

and stopped.

"Myron Matthews," the red-haired girl said. "It *is* you! I heard there was some little kid snooping around the lunchroom."

I tried to speak, but no words came out. The raspberry jam in my mouth had turned to glue.

Sarah "Smasher" McGintley stood in front of me.

"Why are you snooping around West Meadows Elementary?" Smasher stepped close to our lunch table. She towered over me. "You're far from your detective hero, Max Finder."

Smasher McGintley was cousin to Basher McGintley, the biggest bully back at Central Meadows. The McGintleys liked doing one thing and one thing only: punching. The goal when dealing with bullies, especially the

McGintleys, was to avoid the punching.

"Are you snooping around where you shouldn't be snooping?" Smasher asked.

"Four," I said. "You said the word 'snooping' four times."

Smasher looked like someone had smashed her. "I'll say it four million times if I want to!"

Two kids behind Smasher laughed. They were twins with big ears, flat noses, and small eyes. In detective stories, those are called shifty eyes. Characters with shifty eyes cannot be trusted. Ever.

Smasher smacked her fist on our lunch table. "I'll say this, too, Myron Matthews, kid detective: keep your snooping away from me. Do you hear me?"

"I hear you," I said. "You are standing very close and you spoke very loudly. How could I not hear you?"

Smasher growled.

"No problem, Smasher." Hajrah stuffed the rest of her lunch into her bag. "We were just talking about dropping the whole case."

"No, we weren't," I said, watching her stuff my lunch into my bag. "I said that we—"

"You said we have better things to do, like go outside and play!" said Hajrah, even though I was speaking. She hopped up from the table and yanked me by my collar. I got up and followed her out of the lunchroom.

She didn't slow down until we were outside.

"Why did you lie to Smasher?" I said. "I'm not stopping the investigation!"

"I know that. And you know that," Hajrah said. "But we don't want Smasher to know that. She seemed pretty upset you were investigating the mystery of the stolen snacks."

"You think she's involved?"

Hajrah tugged on a loose strand of hair. "If there's sneaky stuff happening at school, you can bet Smasher McGintley is behind it."

"I know," I said. "I met Smasher in my old neighborhood. Her cousin is Basher. He's a bully."

"Yep, stay clear of the McGintleys! That's my rule."

"Is that why you told her we were dropping the case? Just so we could investigate the case?"

"Exactly!" Hajrah said. "Speaking of investigating, what is Mr. V. doing by that tree?"

Hajrah jogged to the far side of the schoolyard. A large tree lay on its side on the muddy ground, with broken branches scattered about.

A man with a bushy mustache popped up from behind the tree's thick trunk.

"Watch yourself, kids!" he said. "Go play somewhere else."

"We're not playing, Mr. V.," Hajrah said. "We're investigating."

Mr. V. is the school caretaker. I met him last Tuesday, when I visited the school for the first time. He wore a thick blue jacket with the crest of the school on the front. He held a small saw in his hand and had flecks of wood stuck in his mustache.

"Why are you cutting the tree?" I said.

Mr. V. chuckled. "Is that what you're investigating? It's Myron, isn't it?"

"We're actually investigating the stolen snacks, Mr. V.," said Hajrah.

Mr. V. shook his head at the mention of the crime.

"A real shame. And on the first day of school. Who would do such a thing?"

"That's what we're trying to find out," I said.

"Hey!" Hajrah suddenly sounded very worried. "This is Smoky's tree!"

"Who's Smoky?"

"She's a raccoon who lives in this tree,"

Hajrah said. "When the weather is nice, my dad and I come here to play soccer after dinner. Sometimes we see Smoky coming down from her tree to look for food."

"And now someone has cut down her tree," I said.

"It wasn't cut down," Mr. V. said. "It fell in last night's storm."

A big thunderstorm started just as I was going to bed last night. Alicia said she hoped the storm would blow away the school. That way, we wouldn't have to go in the morning. I told her it was impossible for a school to blow away. A building like a school can be blown down if the winds are strong enough, but it will never blow away. A building is not like a leaf on a breeze.

I tried to explain this to Alicia, but she just

closed her bedroom door. That's sisters for you.

"Poor thing," Hajrah said. "I hope Smoky is okay."

"The storm took down this tree and ripped a big hole in the roof of the school." Mr. V. pointed to a part of the school covered with a large plastic sheet.

"That's near room 15," I said.

"You got that right, Myron," Mr. V. said. "The wind pulled away some of the roof over the kitchen. I just got it covered this morning before school started."

The recess bell rang.

Hajrah ran toward the school. She stopped when she saw that I wasn't following her.

"Come on, Myron," she said. "Recess is over. Time for our afternoon class in our new room!"

A *new* new classroom with a *new* new teacher and *new* new students.

I *still* did not like new things.

CHAPTER 6

My afternoon classroom smelled like vanilla
cupcakes. I do not like vanilla. I like chocolate.
No one was eating cupcakes. Hajrah said the
smell came from Ms. Chu's perfume. I don't
know why someone would want to wear
perfume that made her smell like a dessert.

I tried to not to think about Ms. Chu's
perfume. It was hard. My mom says that
when something gets in my head, I can't let
go of it. This is true. If something is bothering
me, I think and think and think about it until

my brain feels like it's going to explode. That would never happen, though. Exploding brains happen only in movies, on TV, and in video games.

Getting things stuck in your head is not always bad. It's a good skill for a detective. I could not stop thinking about who could be the Snack Snatcher. This is a good thing because I knew I would solve the mystery. It would stay stuck in my head until I caught the thief.

There were nineteen kids in my afternoon class. Ten boys and nine girls. And one teacher, Ms. Chu. She was a girl, too, but not really. She was a grown-up, so she was a woman.

Ms. Chu was nice, but she looked tired. I wondered why she would be so tired on the first day of school.

This classroom had more stuff in it. Desks, tables, books, and a few computers. Ms. Chu even let me and Hajrah sit together.

"Boys and girls," Ms. Chu said when we were all at our desks, "this afternoon we will be doing math."

"Is it a test?" a boy with spiky hair said. "We can't have a math test on first day of school, can we?"

"Relax, Hamid. It's not a test. It's just a few questions so I know where we all are on our math journey."

I didn't groan. I like math. Numbers will

always tell you what they mean. They're like a reliable witness in a mystery. A reliable witness is someone who saw the crime and tells you the truth. I needed a reliable witness to this morning's snack theft. Hajrah didn't see anything because she was in the closet. I could not call her a reliable witness. I needed someone else.

Ms. Chu handed out a piece of paper with math questions on it. She put one on my desk.

"If you need help with these questions, Myron, just let me know," she said.

When Ms. Chu stood close, it felt like I was inside a vanilla cupcake. I did not want to breathe or I might be sick from the smell. But if I didn't breathe, I would die. Dying is worse than being sick. But if I was sick, I could not solve the mystery of the Snack

Snatcher. I breathed through my mouth. Thankfully, Ms. Chu's perfume didn't taste like vanilla cupcakes.

The math questions were not hard, but I still had a hard time answering them. I couldn't concentrate on the numbers on the page. I had too many other questions to answer. Questions about the Snack Snatcher.

What had the thief done with the morning snack? Were there any witnesses? Who else was in the kitchen this morning? Why are two boys standing in front of my desk?

Smasher's two friends from the lunchroom stared down at me with their shifty eyes. I'd heard Ms. Chu call their names during attendance: Cameron and Carter.

"Working hard, Snoop?" said Cameron.

"My name is not Snoop," I said. "Please

don't call me that."

"We'll call you whatever we like, Snoop," said Carter.

Hajrah stopped working on her math questions.

"Get lost, guys," she said. "We're busy."

Cameron leaned in close to me. Very close. He brought his face into my personal space. My brain began to buzz.

"You two better not be thinking about those missing snacks," Cameron said. "If Smasher finds out you've been snooping, she won't be happy."

My brain buzzed louder. That was not good. The buzzing was a warning to my body that I was getting upset. Sometimes when I get upset, I cannot control what I say or do. I tried to tell Cameron and Carter to go away, but the

words would not come out.

But Hajrah had no trouble with words. "We're not snooping!" she said, loud enough for the class to hear. She jumped to her feet. "We're doing our math. Now go away!"

"Boys," Ms. Chu called from her desk. Carter and Cameron jumped at the sound of the teacher's voice. "Back to your seats."

Carter and Cameron looked at me the whole way back to their desks. It was the same look bad guys in movies have when they want to tell the good guys, *I'll get you.*

"Don't worry about those two," Hajrah said. "They've been bullies since kindergarten."

"My rule is to stay away from bullies," I said.

"That's a good rule." Hajrah went back to working on her math questions.

I had questions to answer but they weren't

the ones on my math sheet. Why didn't
Cameron and Carter want us to find the Snack
Snatcher? What had them so worried? Were
they involved? They could be witnesses or
even suspects. I had to find out. That meant
I had to talk to them. But how could I talk
to them and stay away from them at the
same time?

At the end of the day, I waited for Alicia
to pick me up by the school doors. Hajrah
waited with me. Her mom didn't finish work
for another hour, so she went to the daycare
after school.

"We can discuss the case until my sister gets
here," I said.

"Shh! Here comes our number-one suspect."

Glitch came through the doors with the rest of the kids from her afternoon class. She had her backpack over her shoulder and was on her way home. She stopped when she saw us.

"I've been looking for you two," she said.

My brain buzzed again. It is never good to have your number-one suspect looking for you. It usually means she wants to stop you from investigating the mystery. And she won't be very nice about it.

Glitch waited until all the other kids had left.

"I want to hire you," she said.

"Hire us?" Hajrah said.

"Everyone thinks I stole those snacks this morning."

"A logical assumption," I said. "You did steal stuff last year, right?"

Hajrah thumped me on the shoulder. "Myron! That's rude."

"It's not rude," I said. "It's the truth. You told me so yourself, Hajrah."

"Yes, but …" Hajrah's voice got quiet and then her words just stopped.

"It's okay," Glitch said. "I made a mistake last year, but I did *not* take those snacks this morning."

"Why did Principal Rainer talk to you?" I asked.

"Because she thinks I haven't learned my lesson!"

"Principal Rainer thinks you took the snacks?"

"So does everyone else. That's why I need you," Glitch said. "I want you to find out who really took the snacks."

"We'll take the case!" Hajrah shook Glitch's

hand so hard it made the robot buttons on the girl's backpack rattle.

"We're already on the case, Hajrah," I said.

"I know, but now we have an actual client. Just like real detectives!"

She had a point. Detectives always have a client. That's the person they're solving the mystery for.

"Well, detectives," Glitch said, "will you take my case?"

Hajrah nodded.

"My partner thinks it's a good idea," I said. "And so do I."

A horn honked from a blue van in the parking lot.

"That's my dad," Glitch said. "I'll see you in room 15 tomorrow."

She ran to the waiting van, leaving me with my detective partner, a new clue, and a new question. How did Glitch go from being our number-one suspect to our number-one client?

CHAPTER 7

That night I lost Sherlock Holmes. He's a world-famous detective. And I lost him.

I did not lose an actual person called Sherlock Holmes. That would be impossible. Sherlock Holmes is not real. He's a character from mystery stories.

The Sherlock Holmes I lost was made of paper. He was part of my project, and I needed to find him.

"Did you look under the table?" Mom said.

I looked under the table. No Sherlock.

"Did you leave it in your schoolbag?" she asked.

I looked in my schoolbag. No Sherlock.

The project is called the *Mystery-o-pedia*. It is not for school. It is for me, and it is not finished. When it's done, it will be an

encyclopedia that lists all the famous detectives from books and their greatest mysteries. That is why it's called the *Mystery-o-pedia*.

Right now, it was a mess of paper and glue on our kitchen table, and my brain was buzzing.

"Take a break, Myron," Mom said. "The *Mystery-o-pedia* can wait."

She rubbed the back of my head. That usually made the buzz go away. The doctors say my brain feels like it's buzzing when I get frustrated. But it wasn't the missing Sherlock that was upsetting me. It was Hajrah and Glitch.

Hajrah was my detective partner. Glitch was our client. In all the stories in my *Mystery-o-pedia*, the partner and the client work with the detective to solve the mystery. But the mystery of the Snack Snatcher was different. My partner and my client were also my suspects.

Glitch stole stuff last year. Did she steal the snacks this year? Did she hire us to get us off her trail?

Hajrah was hiding in the kitchen closet when the snacks were stolen. She said she didn't see the thief. Was she telling the truth?

Worst of all, if Hajrah was the Snack Snatcher, I would lose my detective partner and my only friend at my new school. I was just beginning to like having a detective partner.

Alicia came into the kitchen. She got some orange juice from the fridge.

"Why does Columbo have a man in a funny hat stuck to his ear?" she asked.

Columbo is a basset hound. His ears droop to the floor and his body is long and thin like a sausage. Columbo belongs to the whole family, but he likes me best. I change his water and take him for walks. Alicia just makes fun of him. But I know she likes him, too.

A paper cutout of a detective hung from Columbo's left ear.

"Sherlock Holmes!" I plucked up the detective, then I hugged Columbo. He licked my face. It was wet and warm. I don't like wet things on my face, but it's different when the wet thing is Columbo licking.

The buzzing in my head disappeared.

"The picture fell from the table after I put glue on it," I explained to Alicia. "The glue stuck the paper to Columbo's ears when he walked by."

"I always knew his big ears would be good for cleaning the floors," Alicia said.

"And for solving mysteries!" I hugged Columbo again. I glued the picture of Sherlock Holmes into the *Mystery-o-pedia*. There were dog hairs stuck to the picture.

I didn't mind. They were Colombo's hairs. He deserved a spot in my book for solving the mystery of the missing detective.

The next morning I was late getting to school. It wasn't my fault. I'm always on time. I do not like being late. Alicia thinks it's cool to be late for things. She says it's called being "fashionably late." Detectives don't care about fashion.

I got to school just as the last entry bell rang. I hurried to room 15. No one was there.

"Myron! Come here, quick!" Hajrah called to me from down the hall. She was outside the kitchen. She wasn't alone. Mr. Harpel was there, talking quietly to Mrs. Peterson. Glitch was there, too. She stared at something inside the kitchen.

I joined them at the door.

"The Snack Snatcher struck again!" Hajrah said.

The kitchen was a mess. Packages of food were ripped open and tossed around the room. Red pizza sauce had spilled across the counter. Mr. V. was in the middle of it all with a mop, cleaning up the mess.

"I don't know how he got into the school," Mr. V. said. "I'm always the first one here in the morning. I leave the front door unlocked after I get here. That way, teachers can get in if they arrive early. But this mess was here before I even unlocked the doors."

"I can't cook like this!" Mrs. Peterson said. "This is the second morning I come in to find a mess in my kitchen."

"I'm cleaning it up as fast as I can," Mr. V. said.

"Oh, I didn't mean that, Mr. V.," Mrs. Peterson said. "You're working too hard. Cleaning up fallen trees, patching holes in the roof. And now this! It's the last thing you need."

The last thing *I* needed was Mr. V. mopping up valuable clues.

"I asked them to wait," Hajrah said to me. "But Mrs. Peterson needs a clean kitchen to start making lunch for everyone."

"We'll never solve this mystery if we can't investigate the crime scenes," I said.

"I know," agreed Hajrah. "I got the scoop from Mrs. Peterson. This crime is different from yesterday's."

"It looks like the same mess as yesterday."

"Almost the same mess," Hajrah said. "This time, the kitchen was ruined *before* Mrs. Peterson arrived at school. The cupboards were open and food was knocked off the shelves."

"So the thief struck at night this time. After everyone had left."

"But how did the thief get into the school?" Hajrah asked.

"If only I had seen the crime scene before Mr. V. mopped it up," I said. "Now we'll never know."

Glitch came up behind me. "Never say never when Glitch and her cameras are around! I took some photos before Mr. V. got the mess totally cleaned up."

"Those are pictures I want to see," I said.

"We could look at them in the classroom," Mr. Harpel suggested.

Twenty minutes later, we were sitting on the carpet looking at photos of spilled pasta sauce projected onto the classroom's whiteboard. Jordan wandered in. "Is that what Mrs. Peterson is making us for lunch today?"

Hajrah bounced over to make room for him

on the carpet. "It's our latest crime scene!"

Glitch's photos showed what the kitchen looked like just as Mr. V. started cleaning up the mess. It was better than nothing.

"A lot of stuff is knocked over," Hajrah said. "The thieves are very clumsy."

"Maybe they wanted to make a mess," Glitch said.

"Maybe they wanted to tell Mrs. Peterson they didn't like her cooking," Jordan said.

The others kept tossing around their ideas, but I wasn't really listening. I was looking. Glitch's photos showed the Snack Snatcher's mess from different angles. Mr. V. had mopped up most of the pizza sauce from the floor. But there were still red splatters on the walls and even on the small window looking out to the school parking lot.

"Wait!" I said.

All eyes turned to me.

"What is it, Myron?" Hajrah asked.

I walked right up to the whiteboard and pointed to a red splotch on the window.

"The thief really splashed the pizza sauce far," Glitch said.

"That's not pizza sauce." I shook my head. "It's a different kind of red."

"It's auburn," Jordan said. "I have paints that color at home. It's great for painting people who have red hair."

Glitch squinted at the red splotch on the screen. "That's somebody's hair?"

"Somebody with *red* hair," I said. "Somebody who was very worried about us snooping around the school."

Hajrah jumped to her feet. "Smasher!"

CHAPTER 8

The daycare was a disaster. The tables were covered in half-eaten food, spilled milk, and sticky red jam.

"Looks like the Snack Snatcher was here," I said.

"Not the Snack Snatcher," Hajrah said. "Little kids and lunch. Always a messy combo. This is where the kindergarten kids eat."

"It looks like there was more throwing than eating."

Hajrah shrugged. "That's little kids for you."

She was right. When Sofia eats dinner, most of it ends up in her hair or on the floor.

The rest of the daycare wasn't messy. Board games and toys were stacked on shelves along the walls. A bright red-and-green carpet stretched in one corner, near bins of books. Hajrah and other kids came here every day before and after school while their parents were working.

We were working, too. Not schoolwork. Detective work. We had a witness to interview: Lindsay, the daycare assistant.

I had done a lot of thinking since yesterday. Most of it about Hajrah. She said she didn't see the Snack Snatcher because she was eating licorice in the closet in the kitchen. But she did hear a noise. She thought it was Lindsay from the daycare looking for her. If Lindsay went into the kitchen looking for Hajrah, then maybe she saw the Snack Snatcher.

A large woman in a food-stained apron came through the door on the far side of the daycare. She started wiping the tables with a wet cloth.

"Hi, Lindsay!" Hajrah said.

Lindsay jumped and nearly dropped her cloth. She smiled when she saw us in the doorway.

"Hajrah! You startled me." Lindsay looked to me. "Who's your friend?"

"This is Myron. We want to interview you."

"Interview me?" Lindsay said. She checked herself in the mirror in the dress-up corner. "Is it for TV? Should I get my hair done?"

"Not that kind of interview." Hajrah giggled. "Myron and I are detectives, and we need to talk to you."

"This sounds serious. What did I do?"

"It's not what you did but what you saw," I said.

"What I saw when?"

"Monday morning before school," I said. "When you went to the kitchen looking for Hajrah."

"I was hiding in the closet," said Hajrah. She stared at a piece of mushed sandwich on the ground. "Eating licorice."

"Ah, yes. Hajrah and her morning licorice." Lindsay's voice grew serious. "You know your mom doesn't like you eating candy in the morning."

"I know, but I can't help it! It's so delicious."

"That's why it's best to save it for lunch. But this doesn't answer Myron's question."

Lindsay turned to me. "I'm sorry, Myron, but I didn't see anything in the kitchen on Monday morning because I didn't go into the kitchen. I heard all the racket and poor Mrs. Peterson screaming, but I had my hands full in here with the children. Besides, I saw Principal Rainer run to the kitchen, so I thought it was all taken care of."

"You're sure you didn't go into the kitchen?" Hajrah said. "I know I heard someone while I was in the closet."

"It wasn't me." Lindsay started wiping the tables again. "Sorry I can't be of more help to you, detectives."

The interview was over. If Lindsay didn't go into the kitchen, then she wasn't a witness. She could not help us catch the Snack Snatcher. Hajrah and I turned to leave.

"Wait a minute!" Lindsay stood up straight. The cloth dangled from her hand as if she'd forgotten it was there. "I did see someone leaving the kitchen first thing Monday morning, before anyone else arrived."

I pulled my notebook out of my backpack. "Can you describe them?"

Lindsay shook her head. "Hard to say. I

90

didn't get a good look. But I remember the person wore a black jacket with a big red ball on the back."

I wrote the description in my notebook.

"Sounds like the logo for the Meadows Fireballs," Hajrah said.

"The Meadows what?" I said.

"The Fireballs. You know, the professional soccer team?"

I didn't know. I don't pay attention to sports.

"Maybe that's who you need to interview next," Lindsay said. She went back to wiping down the tables.

Hajrah was already on her way outside.

"Where are you going?" I asked.

"Outside before recess is over," she said without slowing down. "It's chilly out there."

I ran to catch up with her.

"What does the weather have to do with our case?"

Hajrah stopped at the doors. "What do people wear when it's cold outside, Myron?"

She bounced on the spot like she had to pee really badly.

"Jackets!" I said. Now I knew why she was in such a rush to get outside. "You want to look for kids wearing Meadows Fireballs jackets."

"One could be a suspect," Hajrah said.

"One could be the Snack Snatcher!" I said.

"Exactly. Let's go jacket hunting before it gets warmer."

CHAPTER 9

That afternoon, Ms. Chu had us all working on "All About Me" acrostic poems. An acrostic poem uses the first letter of a word to start each line of the poem.

Hajrah had no trouble creating her poem:

H appy
A wesome
J umpy
R unning
A lways
H ooray!

This was my poem:

M ysteries
Y
R
O
N

I'm not very good at writing poems.

I was also too busy thinking about the Meadows Fireballs.

Apparently, they are a big soccer team in town. I didn't know anything about them. I'm not a big soccer fan. I'm not a big any-sports fan. I don't see the point in kicking a ball across a field. It would be much easier to pick it up and carry it.

The person Lindsay saw leaving the kitchen on Monday morning was wearing a Meadows

Fireballs jacket. That is a clue. I am a big fan of clues.

Unfortunately, a lot of kids at our school are big fans of the Meadows Fireballs. I stared at my notebook on my desk. I had made a mark for every person we saw wearing a Fireballs jacket at recess. I counted the marks three times. Each time, the answer made me want to give up this case.

"Twenty-seven," I said to Hajrah. "That's how many kids were wearing Fireballs jackets."

"Everybody loves that team." Hajrah colored the letters in her poem with crayons. "They won

the provincial finals last season."

"We don't have time to interview twenty-seven suspects."

"Having that many suspects doesn't help us," Hajrah said.

"It might," I said. "Sometimes the best clues are not helpful at first. I think this might be that type of clue."

Hajrah looked at the paper on my desk and smiled.

"File it away, then, detective, and get to work on your poem. Right now it stinks."

I knew Hajrah was joking. I also knew she was right.

A shadow fell across my paper. Cameron and Carter crowded around my desk. They had seen us counting Fireballs jackets at recess, but they must have been on a bully break. Now break time was over. Cameron jabbed his finger at my poem.

"You spelled your name wrong," he said.

Carter laughed through his nose.

"Yeah," he said. "You spell it S-N-O-O-P."

Words raced through my head. Not nice words. I took a deep breath and kept the words inside. For now.

Hajrah didn't keep her words inside.

"Go jump in the compost bin!" she said. "Leave us alone."

"We'll leave you alone when you stop snooping around the kitchen," Cameron said.

Carter held one of my purple crayons in both hands. He leaned in close. His breath smelled like tuna fish.

"Stay away from the kitchen," he said. Then he snapped the crayon in two.

"Boys!" The two goons jumped at the sound of Ms. Chu's voice. "Leave Myron and Hajrah alone and get back to work."

"We were just borrowing a crayon," Cameron said.

"No, they weren't!" I said. Cameron was trying to trick Ms. Chu. I couldn't keep the words in my head any longer. "They came over here and broke my crayon."

I held up the broken purple crayon for Ms. Chu to see.

"It's true, Ms. Chu!" Hajrah said.

"Boys," she said. "Meet me at my desk. Now."

When a teacher says "meet me at my desk," it's because you are in trouble.

"You'll regret this, Snooper," Cameron said.

"Yeah, this isn't over," hissed Carter.

Hajrah stuck her tongue out at both of them. She did it so fast that Ms. Chu didn't notice.

Cameron and Carter met Ms. Chu at her desk. She spoke to them so quietly I couldn't hear, but I knew they were getting in trouble.

"Smasher is totally the Snack Snatcher," Hajrah whispered to me. "That's why she wants us to stay away from the kitchen."

"She's probably planning to strike again,"

I said. "I wish we could be there."

"We could hide in the closet like I did!"

"My mom would not let me stay in a closet overnight."

"We don't have to," Hajrah said. "We come in early, like I did on Monday, and hide in the closet before the thief strikes!"

"We'll be too late," I said. "The Snack Snatcher can get into the school any time. Even before Mr. V. gets here."

Hajrah went back to coloring her poem, but I knew she was still thinking about our problem.

"We need a set of eyes there all night," she said.

"Like a camera," I said.

Hajrah looked up from her poem. She had a big smile on her face. I could tell it was a real smile because her eyes kind of sparkled.

"And we know someone with a camera."

"Glitch!" I said. And I was smiling, too.

CHAPTER 10

I raced to room 15 right after the end-of-day bell.

Mr. Harpel was still there. He agreed to help us.

Hajrah had helped me finish my poem and then we'd come up with a plan. My job was to talk to Mr. Harpel. Her job was to find Glitch.

"Here we are!" Hajrah ran into the classroom. She was out of breath and smiling.

Glitch followed her into the room. She was smiling, too.

"Hajrah told me about your plan to catch the thief," Glitch said. "I have just the stuff to get it all set up."

"I'll talk to Mr. V. and make sure he's okay with everything," Mr. Harpel said. He picked up the phone on the wall and called the office.

Glitch rummaged around the shelves near her table. She pulled out a long black cable, a little box with lights on it, and a fat roll of tape. She put it all on the table, then she pulled her camera from her backpack and turned to us.

"Ready to catch the Snack Snatcher?" she asked.

"More than ready!" Hajrah jumped and clapped her hands. I didn't understand how she could be "more" than ready. You are either ready or you are not ready.

Twenty minutes later, Glitch's camera was definitely ready. Mr. V. let us set it all up.

He even met us in the kitchen to help.

When it was all done, the camera rested on a high shelf in a corner of the kitchen. It was pointed to the middle of the room. The black cable stuck out from the back of the camera. It was taped to the wall and ran all the way to the door. The cable plugged into the little box with lights. The box was stuck to the top of the doorframe.

"The little box is a sensor," Glitch said. "When the door is opened, the sensor sends a signal to the camera. The signal tells the camera to start taking pictures."

"Very smart," Mr. Harpel said.

"I put a wide-angle lens on the camera," Glitch said. "That way, the whole kitchen will be in the picture."

"Including the window?" I asked.

"Do you think that's how the thief got in?" Mr. Harpel peered at the window.

"Impossible," said Mr. V. "I make sure all the windows are locked every night. And I know that window was locked when the Snack Snatcher got in here last night."

"So how did the thief get into the kitchen?" Mr. Harpel said.

Glitch pointed to her camera. "I guess we'll find out tomorrow morning."

I did not sleep much that night. My mind was buzzing. It was a good buzzing. My brain buzzed with ideas about the Snack Snatcher and Glitch's camera. If it all worked, I would have this case solved by morning recess.

The next morning, I woke up early and left for school as soon as I could. I had to get there before the other students. Alicia woke up early, too, and came with me. It was still dark outside as we walked to school. She yawned fifteen times on the way there.

"I haven't been up this early since I was a toddler." She yawned again. Number sixteen.

Alicia used to help me solve mysteries all the time when we were younger. Now all she wants to do is talk to her friends and listen to music on her headphones. It was chilly this early in the morning, but walking to school with my sister I wasn't cold at all.

"Thank you for coming with me," I said. "It's the only way Mom would let me go to school so early."

"No worries, little brother," she said. "It's

been too long since I helped our family detective solve his latest mystery."

The school was quiet and dark when we got there. Only a few lights were on inside this early in the morning. We walked up the path to the front doors. There was no one else around.

"Looks like we're the first to arrive," I said.

"That makes me second!" Glitch appeared at the bottom of the path. She walked up to join us. A minivan pulled into the parking lot. Hajrah jumped out and waved.

"And Hajrah is number three," I said.

Hajrah's mom honked the horn, waved to us, and drove away. Hajrah ran up the path to us.

"I told my mom you were looking after us, Alicia," she said when she reached us.

"She's taken her babysitting course, so she is

qualified," I said.

"My babysitting doesn't usually start so early." Alicia yawned again. Number seventeen.

We were early, and that was the plan. School didn't start for a while, but we had a lot to see before then.

"Do you think the Snack Snatcher returned?" Glitch said.

"Hopefully your camera will answer that," Hajrah said.

Mr. V. appeared at the door.

"Come on in! It's not locked," he said. "I've been here about an hour. Mr. Harpel is here, too."

Mr. V. went back inside. Alicia went in after him. Glitch followed my sister. I grabbed Hajrah's sleeve before she should go any farther.

I pointed to Glitch. She walked away from us down the hall. She wore a black jacket. On the back was a red soccer ball that looked like a fireball.

"Meadows Fireballs!" Hajrah hissed.

I tried to go into the school, but my feet wouldn't move. My brain was too busy trying to figure out what I just saw.

"Glitch is the Snack Snatcher!" Hajrah said under her breath.

But why would Glitch help us catch the Snack Snatcher if *she* was the Snack Snatcher? Why would she hire us to clear her name if she was really guilty? I was still working on this when we got to the kitchen.

Mr. V. stood outside the door with Glitch and Alicia. Mr. Harpel and Principal Rainer were there, too.

"I wish all our students showed up this early for school," said Principal Rainer when she saw us.

"We're here to catch the Snack Snatcher," I said.

"That's a good thing," Mr. Harpel said. "They struck again."

Inside the kitchen was a mess. Food was scattered across the floor.

"But this time we got the thief on camera, right?" Hajrah said.

Mr. Harpel held up a small box with wires on it.

It was Glitch's door sensor. We'd left it stuck to the doorframe. It was crushed flat and the wires were bent.

"Someone sabotaged our camera trap!" Glitch said.

"I don't know what happened," Mr. V. said. "Your equipment was fine when I locked up the school last night."

"Now we'll never catch the Snack Snatcher!" Hajrah said.

She was right. The Snack Snatcher was one step ahead of us. It was as if the thief had been in on the plan the whole time.

I looked over at Glitch. She was trying to put the door sensor back together. She did look sad. But all I could really see was the flaming soccer ball on her back.

CHAPTER 11

This mystery was a mess. The Snack Snatcher had struck for the third time. Our plan to snap photos of the thief in action was crushed like the door sensor. And our client looked more guilty every minute. But for this first time since taking this case, I was happy.

"Why are you smiling, Myron?" asked Principal Rainer.

"There is food everywhere," I said.

"We see that," Mr. Harpel said. "Poor Mr. V. has to clean it all up again."

I turned to Mr. V. "But you haven't started cleaning yet. Right?"

Mr. V. shook his head. "Haven't had time! I went to the roof when I got here this morning. The hole caused by the storm is still leaking."

"Perfect," I said.

"How is that perfect?" Hajrah said. "The Snack Snatcher struck again, but we have no photos and still no idea who is behind the messes. We have nothing."

"Wrong," I said. "Finally, we have an untouched crime scene."

The first two times the Snack Snatcher struck, I arrived at the crime scene after someone had already walked through the evidence or started cleaning it up. This time it was untouched. A perfect mess, ready to be investigated. I stepped carefully into the kitchen.

And that's when I saw them. Tracks through the spilled pizza sauce. A little path of tiny footprints. They looked almost like little handprints. Four fingers and a  thumb with long nails. There were dozens of them. They went through the sauce, across the floor, and up the wall. They led to a small air vent high in the ceiling.

A movement outside the window caught my eye. Hajrah stood beside me, and I knew she had seen it, too. She tugged on the hem of her jacket. Her brain worked through the same clues until her eyes lit up.

"Outside," she whispered, looking at me.

I nodded, then turned to the others.

"Everyone meet me outside! And, Mr. V., could you bring your ladder, please?"

We gathered outside the school right in front of the kitchen window. Mr. V. arrived with his ladder. Glitch looked through the glass into the kitchen.

"What's this all about, Myron?" she said. "The mess is inside, not out here."

"Very true, Glitch," I said.

Hajrah stood by a bush near the little group of trees that ran along the side of the school.

"But the answer to this mystery is out here." Hajrah turned to the bush as if she was speaking to it. "Isn't that right?"

"Don't worry," I said to the bush. "You can come out. We won't hurt them."

"You promise?" said a voice from the other side of the branches.

"We promise," Hajrah said.

"Okay," said the voice. A red-faced and auburn-haired figure stood up from her hiding spot.

"Smasher!" Mr. Harpel said.

Smasher stepped out of the bushes. She wore the same black jacket as Glitch. As she climbed over the hedge, I saw what was on the back: a red soccer ball that looked like a fireball.

"You stole the morning snacks!" Principal Rainer said.

"No, I didn't," Smasher said.

"She's right," said Hajrah. "Smasher isn't the Snack Snatcher."

Principal Rainer let out a big sigh. "Then

who is?" she asked.

"They are."

I pointed to the roof near the kitchen. A plastic sheet covered the hole caused by the storm. A small head covered in brown fur with a large black patch over the eyes peered out from under the sheet.

"Smoky!" Hajrah squealed. "You're alive!"

Two more furry heads poked out from under the sheet.

"And she's not alone," said Glitch.

"Principal Rainer," I said, "meet the Snack Snatchers."

CHAPTER 12

The afternoon sun beamed down on the
busy schoolyard. Around me, every kid ran,
chased, screamed, and enjoyed recess. Every
kid except me, that is.

Smasher McGintley had me cornered.
Cameron and Carter kept a lookout.

"You think you're smart, don't you,
detective?" Smasher growled. "You think you
have me all figured out?"

"Not at all," I said. "You're a very complex
person."

Who would have guessed that the meanest kid in school had a soft spot for a family of homeless raccoons?

Once we'd lured Smasher out of the bushes, she'd confessed to everything.

She'd arrived at school early on the first day. She saw Smoky the raccoon and her babies making the mess in the kitchen. The raccoons grabbed the morning snacks and dragged them into the air vent. They had been hiding there ever since the storm knocked down their tree in the schoolyard.

Raccoons are nocturnal, so Smoky and her cubs slept in the roof during the day. They came out the next night and looked for more food in the kitchen.

Smasher didn't tell anyone about the raccoons. She came by the kitchen in the morning before school to check they were okay.

She was peeking through the window when Glitch took a photo of the kitchen the second time the raccoons made a mess. That's why we saw the bit of red hair in the photo. Then she spotted Glitch's motion sensor when she opened the kitchen door this morning. She reached around the doorway and knocked the sensor to the ground, wrecking it before the camera took any photos.

And now she was going to wreck me because I'd figured it all out.

"You're just a twerp detective," she said. "I warned you to stop snooping around."

"But it all worked out in the end, didn't it?" I said. "No one thinks you're the Snack Snatcher. In fact, Principal Rainer is impressed

that you helped the raccoons. She said you
have a kind heart."

That made Smasher even more mad. Behind
her, Cameron and Carter snickered. She glared
at her goons. Their smiles vanished. Smasher
turned back to me.

"You'd better not repeat those words to
anyone else. Got it?"

I nodded real fast to show her I got it.

"This isn't over, Myron Matthews," she said. "Keep me out of your mysteries."

She turned to go. Her two snickering goons followed.

"Myron!" Hajrah's head popped out from around the corner. "There you are! I've been looking for you. Hurry up! You're going to miss the fun."

"Stand back, kids." Mr. Harpel ushered us away from the tall oak tree on the far side of the schoolyard.

Mr. V. and a woman from the Animal Rescue Service placed a large cage at the foot of the tree. Smoky and her two babies peered out from behind the bars.

"They look so scared," Hajrah said.

"They're just a little nervous," said the woman from the Animal Rescue Service. Her name was Melanie. She'd helped Mr. V. get Smoky and her babies down from the roof. "They'll be fine once we get them to their new home."

Glitch moved around to the other side of the tree with her camera.

"Everyone smile!" she said as she snapped another photo.

"Ready?" Mr. V. asked.

We all stood back and Melanie opened the cage door. Smoky came out first. Her cubs followed her. The mama raccoon sniffed her way to the tree and scrambled up the trunk. Her babies were right behind her. High above us, the raccoon family climbed along the branches.

"I think they like their new home!" Hajrah said.

"It will be a new beginning for all of them." Mr. Harpel smiled.

I looked at all of us gathered around the tree—my new teacher and my new friends. And my first new mystery solved. A few days ago, I didn't like any of this new stuff. But I was wrong.

New beginnings weren't so bad after all.

Acknowledgments

Every detective relies on a great team, and writers are no different. This book would not have been written without the support of Melanie McBride and our many chats about life, the universe, and camping. Thank you for everything, Mel. A very big thank you to Dr. Jason Nolan, professor of early childhood studies at Ryerson University, who is autistic, for his advice and ongoing guidance around autism, learning, and much more. Any inaccuracies are mine alone.

Mega-mystery thanks to Karen Li for her sharp-eyed and thoughtful editing. Myron and Hajrah became better characters (and detectives!) under her guidance. And finally, thank you to everyone at Owlkids for giving me the chance to explore Whispering Meadows a little more. I'm excited to see where Myron and Hajrah's travels on the west side of town take us all.

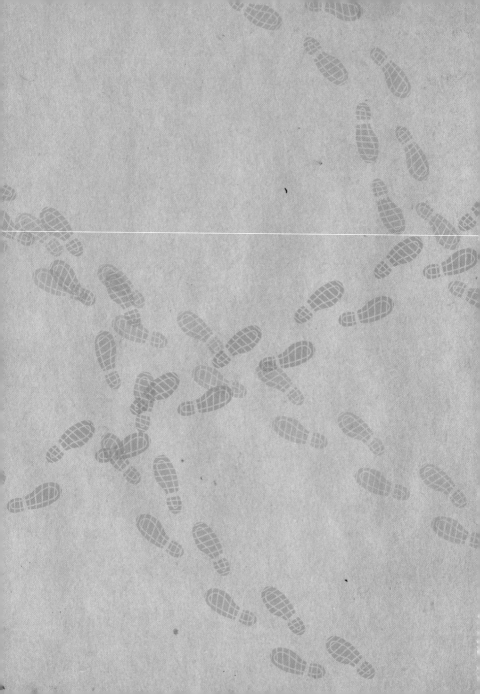